Published by Sweet Cherry Publishing Limited
Unit 36, Vulcan House,
Vulcan Road,
Leicester, LE5 3EF
United Kingdom

First published in the UK in 2021
2021 edition

2 4 6 8 10 9 7 5 3

ISBN: 978-1-78226-435-4

Sherlock Holmes: The Beryl Coronet

Based on the original story from Sir Arthur Conan Doyle,
adapted by Stephanie Baudet.

Cover design by Arianna Bellucci and Amy Booth
Illustrations by Arianna Bellucci

Lexile® code numerical measure L = Lexile® 700L

Guided Reading Level = W

www.sweetcherrypublishing.com

Printed and bound in Turkey
T.IO006

SHERLOCK HOLMES

THE BERYL CORONET

SIR ARTHUR CONAN DOYLE

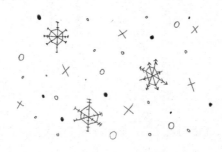

Chapter One

One crisp February morning, I was looking out of the window of our sitting room in Baker Street when I saw something rather odd.

'Holmes!' I said. 'There's a man acting very strangely down in the street. Come and see.'

My friend got up from his armchair and came over to the window. He peered over my shoulder.

The snow from the day before still lay on the sides of the road, shimmering brightly in the winter sun. Down the middle, traffic had ploughed it up into a brown crumbly mush that had frozen again, making it very slippery.

There were very few people outside. One man was walking his dog, a maid carrying loaves of bread was returning from the bakery, and then there was this oddly behaved man.

He must have been about fifty years old and was tall, sturdy and important-looking. He had a strong face and was dressed in a black frock-coat, a shiny top hat and neat, pearl-grey trousers.

He was running along the road, throwing his hands up and down and twisting his face

7

into extraordinary shapes. As he passed each door on Baker Street, he peered at the number and then frowned before running to the next one.

'What on earth can be the matter with him?' I asked.

'We shall soon find out,' said Holmes, rubbing his hands excitedly. 'I think he is coming here.'

'Here?' I asked, surprised.

'Yes. I'm sure he is coming here with a new case for us. I recognise the symptoms – madly running down the street, a look of pure panic on his face,  and peering at the door numbers. He is trying to locate 221B, I am sure. It must be a new case.'

As he spoke, the man rushed to our door, puffing and panting. He rang the doorbell so loudly that the whole house echoed with the noise.

I heard the front door being opened by our housekeeper, Mrs Hudson, and then the sound of footsteps on the stairs.

Seconds later, the sitting room door opened.

'Mr Holmes, sir …' began Mrs Hudson, but the man rushed past her and into the room, still puffing and waving his arms about. I could see now that there was more than panic painted across his face. There was sadness too.

For a while he couldn't speak. He just swayed from side to side and pulled at his hair. Holmes and I helped him into a chair. Then Holmes sat down next to the man and patted his hand.

'He will be fine now,' I said to Mrs Hudson as she left the room.

'You are safe here,' Holmes said
to the man in a soothing tone.
'Take your time. Get your breath
back. Then tell me how I can
help. I shall be very happy to look
into your problem, whatever it is.'

The man sat for a minute or two,
breathing heavily and fighting the
urge to cry. Then he took
out a handkerchief
and mopped his
forehead, before
taking a deep
breath, and turning
to face us.

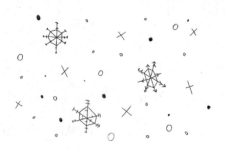

Chapter Two

'You must think I'm mad,' the man said.

'Not at all,' said Holmes, patting the man's hand again. 'I can see that you are facing a problem.'

'I am! It's such a horrible problem that it is enough to send me mad.' The man shook his head, sadly.

'And it is not just me,' he went

on. 'Some very important people may suffer too, unless I can find a solution ... and quickly!'

'Please relax, sir,' said Holmes. 'Tell me who you are and what has happened to you.'

The man took another long, deep breath.

'I am sorry, Mr Holmes and ...' he trailed off.

'Doctor Watson,' I said, quickly introducing myself.

'Well, Doctor Watson and Mr Holmes, my name is Alexander Holder, of Holder and Stevenson

Bank, in Threadneedle Street.'

His name was very well known. He was the senior partner of a very big bank in the City of London. What could have happened to trouble such a rich and important man?

We waited, full of curiosity, until he was ready to tell his story.

'As you know, in the banking business, it's all about making money. One of the best ways of making money is giving loans to businesses – as long as they provide good security. As they will pay back more than they borrow. We have lent a lot of money to businesses, but we also lend large sums of money to families, against the security

Security

When giving out loans, banks ask for a 'security': an expensive item, such as a diamond necklace, a valuable painting or the deed to a house. The borrower gives this item to the bank as a sort of promise to pay back the loaned money on time. If the person pays back the loan, their precious item is returned to them. If not, the bank will keep the item. The more money the person wants to borrow from the bank, the more expensive their 'security' item must be.

of their valuable paintings or books, or their priceless china or jewels.'

We nodded.

'Yesterday morning I was in my office at the bank, doing some paperwork,' Mr Holder continued, 'when there was a knock at my door. It was one of our clerks. He said that there was a visitor who wanted to see me. I was shocked when I saw who it was. It was … well, perhaps I shouldn't tell you. It was someone very famous. I was overwhelmed by the honour of his visit. I tried to tell him so, but he immediately started to talk about business. He seemed in a great hurry.'

'"Mr Holder," he said to me, "I have been told that your bank will lend me some money."

"'P-p-possibly," I stammered.

"'It is absolutely essential that I borrow £50,000 at once," he said.

"'How long do you need the money for?" I asked.

"'Just until next Monday," he said. "Someone owes me a lot of money and they will be paying me on Monday. When they pay me, I can return your money to the bank, with interest, of course. But it's important that I have the £50,000 straightaway."

"'I'll be happy to let you have it now, sir. But I will need some security. Do you have something valuable that you can leave with me, as a promise that you'll pay back the money?" I asked, a little shyly.

"Of course!" he said. He lifted a leather-covered case off his lap. "You must have heard of the Beryl Coronet?"

"It is one of the most precious public possessions in the British Empire," I said, confused by the change of subject.

"Exactly," he replied, with a smirk. Then he carefully opened the case. There, nestled in soft, cream velvet, lay a magnificent crown. The gems in it were clear like diamonds, but with a hint of blue. They glittered like the sea on a summer's day.

"'There are thirty-nine beryls in this," he said, "and the value of the gold around them is enormous. I would say the coronet is worth at

least £100,000 – double the sum
I am borrowing from you. I will
leave this with you as the security
on my loan."

'I took the precious case into
my hands and stared at the
sparkling crown. Then I looked
back at my client.

'"You understand, Mr Holder,
that leaving the coronet here
proves how much I trust you and
your bank," the man said. "I have
heard many good things about
you. Please do not to tell anyone
about this. No one must know that

the coronet is here. Nobody must know about the loan. And you *must* take every possible precaution to guard this precious artifact. There would be a great public scandal if anything happened to it. There are no other beryls like these in the world, and they would be impossible to replace. I leave it with you, trusting that it shall stay safe and sound. I will return to collect it on Monday morning."

'I nodded. Then I called my cashier and ordered him to pay the client £50,000 in cash.

'When I was alone again, with the precious case lying on the table in front of me, I suddenly felt overwhelmed by the responsibility. As my client had said, it would be a national scandal if anything happened to the coronet. I immediately regretted agreeing to take care of it. But it was too late now. So I locked it in the safe and went back to my work.'

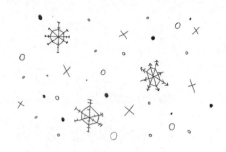

Chapter Three

Mr Holder looked up at us and continued his story. 'When it was time to go home,' he said, 'I took the coronet with me. I could have left it in the bank's safe, but I wanted to keep it close to me at all times. I felt a responsibility for it.

'I decided that I would carry the case to and from work with me each day, so that it would never be out of my sight. Yesterday, I did not relax until I had got home, taken it upstairs and locked it in the desk of my study.'

I looked at Holmes. I couldn't help thinking that this was a strange decision to make. A bank safe seemed a much safer place for the precious crown.

'I felt quite safe having the coronet in my house,' said Mr Holder, as if he had guessed what I was thinking. 'Everyone who lives with me is entirely trustworthy. There's my horse groom, who sleeps above the stable. He's a very pleasant chap. Then I have three maids who have all been with me for quite a few years, and one newer addition: Lucy Parr. She has only worked for me for a few months, but she is a good worker and we are very pleased with her.

'Then there's my family, which is so small that it won't take long to describe. I am a widower and have one son, Arthur. He has been a disappointment to me, Mr Holmes, but I am probably to blame. I spoiled him. When my wife died, he was all I had left to love. I couldn't bear to see the smile fade from his face, so I gave him everything he wanted. Perhaps it would have been better for both of us if I had been stricter, but I did my best.'

Mr Holder paused for a moment, looking down at

his hands regretfully. At that moment, Mrs Hudson came in with a tray of tea. Mr Holder relaxed a little more after he had finished his first cup.

'As I was saying,' he continued, 'Arthur is a little spoilt. I wanted him to follow me into the banking business, but he

was not interested. He was wild and rebellious and could not be trusted to handle large sums of money. He joined a club for gentlemen and made many rich friends. These men had expensive habits – they did a lot of gambling. Arthur lost a lot of money. He came to me again and again asking for more and …' he sighed. 'I would always give it him. But it was never enough.

'He tried several times to leave the club and the dangerous people he'd met there. But each time his friend, Sir George Burnwell, persuaded him to come back.'

I could see a little understanding in Holmes' eyes. We had heard similar stories many times before.

'Arthur brought Sir George Burnwell to the house several times and I saw what he was like. Whatever he says, Arthur will do it. He's a terrible friend to my son. He treats him like a puppet. But he is older than Arthur, well-travelled, very charming and very handsome. Arthur admires him.'

Mr Holder frowned. 'I do not trust him at all, Mr Holmes.

I have seen a certain look in his eye – a flash of evil. My little Mary doesn't agree. But then again, she sees the good in everyone.

'Who is Mary?' asked Holmes.

'Mary is my niece,' said Mr Holder. 'When my brother died five years ago, he left her alone in the world, so I adopted her. She is a sunbeam in my house – sweet, loving, and wonderful at managing the servants. I absolutely adore her and so does

Arthur. In fact, he's been in love with her for years. I only wish she loved him back. She's such a talented young lady.'

Mr Holder stared into the distance and began listing all the many talents of his niece. 'She's a wonderful artist ... a beautiful dancer ... oh, and you must hear her on the piano, she's simply magnificent ...'

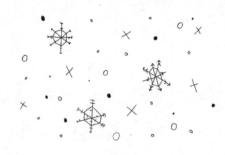

Chapter Four

After three minutes of listening to Mr Holder going on and on about Mary's talents, Holmes' patience finally ran out.

'Back to the story, please, Mr Holder,' Holmes said, waving his hand. 'Did something happen to the coronet?'

I blushed at Holmes' rudeness and looked at him sternly.

'I apologise, gentlemen. I could talk about dear Mary for days,' Mr Holder said, chuckling.

'Where was I? Oh yes. I had locked the coronet in my desk. Then, when we were having coffee in the drawing room after dinner last night, I told Arthur and Mary about the precious treasure that we had under our roof. I didn't, of course, tell them the name of my client. Mary and Arthur were very interested in the famous coronet and wanted to see it, but I thought it best to leave it safely locked away.

"'Where have you put it?"
asked Arthur.

"'In the desk in my study," I said.

"'Well, I hope the house won't be
burgled during the night," he said.

"'What a thing to say, Arthur!
Anyway, the desk is locked, so not

even a burglar would be able to get to it," I said.

'"Oh, any old key will fit that desk," said Arthur. "When I was young, I used to open it with the key of the cellar cupboard."

'Arthur often told little lies and made-up stories, so I didn't take much notice of what he said. But he followed me to my room that night with a very serious look on his face.

'"Um, Father," he said, with his eyes cast down. "Can you let me have two hundred pounds?"

"'No, I cannot!" I answered sharply. "I have been far too generous to you with money."

"'You have been very kind," he said, "but I must have this money. Otherwise I'll never be able to show my face at the club again."

"'That would be a good thing!" I cried.

"'I know you do not like the club, Father, but you wouldn't want me to leave in disgrace, would you? I must get the money somehow. If you will not give it to me, then I must try another way."

I was furious. "You shall not have another penny from me!" I cried.

'Arthur scowled and left the room without uttering another word.

'When he had gone, I unlocked my desk, made sure that the treasure was safe and then locked it again. Then I started to walk around the house to check that all the doors and windows were locked. As I came down the stairs, I saw Mary peering out of the side window in the hall. As I approached her she closed and locked it.

'"Tell me, Uncle," she said,

looking a little worried, "did you give Lucy, the maid, permission to go out tonight?"

"'Certainly not," I said.

"'She came in by the kitchen door just now," said Mary. "I'm sure she has been to the side gate to meet with someone."

"'Really? I will speak to her in the morning," I said. "Are all the doors and windows locked?"

"'Yes, Uncle."

"'Perfect. Goodnight then." I kissed her head and went up to my bedroom, where I was soon asleep.

'I am not a very deep sleeper – I often wake up in the night – and worrying about the coronet made it worse. At about two o'clock in the morning I was woken up by a sound in the house. It sounded like a window being closed.

'Then, to my horror, I suddenly heard the sound of footsteps coming from the next room – my study! I slipped out of bed, my heart pounding, and peeped round the corner of the study door.' Mr Holder stared at us, his eyes wide. 'I couldn't believe what I saw.'

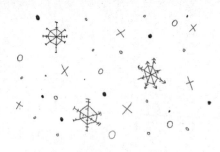

Chapter Five

'"Arthur!" I screamed. "You thief! How dare you touch that coronet!"

'The gaslight was turned half up, as I had left it, and there stood my boy, dressed only in his shirt and trousers, holding the precious crown. He seemed to be trying to twist it with all his strength.

'At my shout, he dropped the coronet onto the desk and

turned pale. I snatched it up and examined it. One of the gold points, with three of the beryls in it, was missing.

"'You villain!" I shouted in rage. "You have destroyed it! You have ruined my name and my business forever! Where is the missing piece that you have stolen?"

"'Stolen?" Arthur cried.

"'Yes, you thief!" I roared, shaking him by the shoulders. "There is a piece missing that contains three gems. You took it!

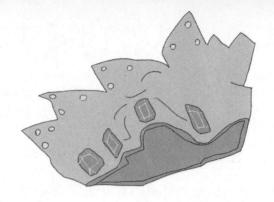

Admit it. Or are you a liar as well as a thief?"

""You have called me enough names," Arthur said angrily. "I will not stand for it any longer. I shall leave the house in the morning and make my own way in the world. I won't say another word about this business."

""You will leave with the police!" I shouted. "You have committed a crime, Arthur."

'"Fine!" he shouted back. "Call the police. Let them find what they can."

'By this time, the whole household had woken up from the shouting. Mary was the first to rush into the room. At the sight of the coronet she gave a little scream and fainted.

'Then I sent one of the maids to fetch the police.

'Arthur was calm now. He stood with his arms folded and asked if I was going to have him charged with theft.

"'I have to," I answered. "The coronet is national property."

"'Please don't have me arrested immediately," he said. "I must leave the house for just five minutes. If you let me, we will both benefit from it."

"'Ha!" I laughed. "Let you leave for five minutes so that you can get away? Or so that you can hide what you have stolen?" I looked at my son's face, which was now set into a scowl. "Arthur, it is not only my reputation at stake here, but also the reputation of the great man who is the guardian of this coronet. He said that any scandal involving it would affect the whole country. It doesn't have to end like this. Just tell me what you have done with the three missing jewels and we can fix this."

Arthur just shook his head.

"'Arthur," I said again, sighing. "You have been caught in the act. If you tell us where the beryls are it shall all be forgiven."

'He turned away from me with a sneer. "Keep your forgiveness for those who ask for it," he said.

'Nothing I said was going to make him confess. There was nothing else I could do but call in the inspector to arrest him.

'Arthur was searched, as was every room in the house, but there was no sign of the missing gems. Arthur would not say another word. He was taken to the police station this morning and locked in a cell.

'I have just come from the station now, Mr Holmes. I beg you to use your skills to unravel this mystery. The police have no clues – they told me to come to you. I need to know what Arthur did with those precious gems.

'You can have as much money as you like. I do not care what it costs. I have already offered a reward of £1,000 for the missing piece. Oh, what shall I do? I have lost the gems, my honour and my son in one night!'

Mr Holder covered his eyes with his

hands as if he were about to cry.

Holmes sat silently for a few minutes staring at the fire, his eyebrows drawn together in a frown.

'Did you have many visitors to the house?' he asked at last.

'Only my business partner and his family, and an occasional friend of Arthur's,' Mr Holder replied. 'Sir George Burnwell has visited several times recently. But no one else, I don't think.'

'Do you go out much?' Holmes asked.

'No. Arthur does, but Mary and I stay at home. Neither of us like socialising much.'

'That is unusual, in a young girl,' I said. 'Usually they like nothing more than balls and dinner parties.'

Mr Holder looked at me. 'Mary is a quiet girl,' he said. 'And she's not so young – she's twenty-four.'

'The crime seems to have shocked her, too. You said she fainted at the scene?' said Holmes.

'She did,' said Mr Holder. 'And she has been crying all day.'

'And are you both sure that your son is guilty?'

'Of course. I saw him with my own eyes with the coronet in his hands.'

'But that isn't absolute proof,' said Holmes. 'Was the rest of the coronet damaged?'

'Yes, it was twisted,' said Mr Holder.

'Don't you think that Arthur could have been trying to straighten it?'

'Bless you!' said Mr Holder,

looking at Holmes with a small smile. 'You are doing what you can to defend him, but I'm afraid we must admit the truth. If he was not stealing the coronet, then what was he doing in my study? If he is innocent, why won't he say so?'

'Hmm,' murmured Holmes, as he ran through the points of the case in his mind. 'What did the police think of the noise that woke you up?'

'They thought that it was Arthur closing his bedroom door.'

'A likely story!' Holmes
scoffed. 'If a man were going to
commit a crime, would he shut
his door loudly enough to wake
the household? I don't think so.'
Holmes paused and then said,
'Where do the police think the
missing jewels are?'

'They do not know. They are
taking apart the furniture, hoping
to find them hidden somewhere.'

Holmes looked at him
shrewdly. 'Have they thought of
looking outside the house?'

'Yes. The whole garden has

been searched thoroughly.'

'My dear sir,' said Holmes, 'I know that this appeared to you to be a simple case, but that is not true.

'Let's think about your theory. You think that your son came out of his bedroom and went into your study, opened the desk, and took out the coronet. Then he broke off a small portion of it, containing three of the gems. Then he went somewhere else and hid that piece so well that no one can find it now. After hiding it, he took the coronet back to your study to put it away again – putting himself in the greatest danger of being discovered. Do you really think that makes sense?'

When Holmes put it like that, it didn't make any sense at all.

'But what else could explain it?' Mr Holder asked, shrugging his shoulders.

'It is our job to find that out,' said Holmes. 'I think, Mr Holder, it is time that we made a trip to your house.'

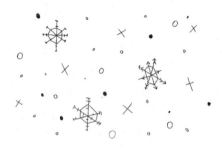

Chapter Six

Holmes hardly spoke at all on the way to Streatham – the south London suburb that Mr Holder called home. He simply sat with his chin on his chest and his hat pulled over his eyes. Mr Holder must have thought that he was falling asleep, but it was clear to me that he was deep in thought.

Mr Holder's house, Fairbank, was a large building that stood a little way back from the road. We entered through a pair of enormous iron gates and walked across the wide driveway, which was bordered with snow-covered grass.

On the right of the drive was a small wooden gate that opened onto a little path. The path cut between two neat hedges and led to the back door, where any deliveries would be taken. On the left of the drive was a lane that I assumed led to the stables. This was a public path, although it didn't look as though it was used much.

When we arrived at the front door, Holmes left us and went off on his own – across the front of the house and along the deliveryman's path.

Mr Holder and I went into the dining room and waited in front of the fire for Holmes to return. I had just managed to shake the brisk chill of the day off me, when the door opened and a young lady came in. She was tall and slim with dark hair and very pale skin. Her lips were pale too, but her eyes were red and swollen with crying.

She seemed even more upset than Mr Holder had been when he came into our rooms earlier. Ignoring me, she went straight to Mr Holder and took his hand.

'Have you told the police to release Arthur, Uncle?' she asked.

'No, no, Mary. It must be investigated thoroughly,' said Mr Holder.

'But I am sure he is innocent!' said Mary. 'I know he has done no harm. You will be very sorry to have acted so harshly.'

'If he is innocent, why didn't he say so?' asked Mr Holder.

'Perhaps he was too angry that you suspected him,' she said.

'I don't just suspect him. I saw him with the coronet in his hands.'

Mary shook her head, looking on the verge of tears. 'He must have just picked it up to look at it,' she insisted. 'Please take my word for it. He is innocent. Please tell the police to let him go. It's dreadful to think of poor Arthur in prison!'

'I cannot do that until the gems are found, Mary,' said Mr Holder. 'Your fondness for Arthur blinds you. I shall not hush things up and pretend this didn't happen. In fact, I have brought a gentleman over from Baker Street to look into it.'

Mary turned to face me. 'This gentleman?' she asked.

'No, this is his friend, Doctor Watson. Mr Holmes wished us to leave him alone. He is probably round in the stable lane now.'

'The stable lane?' She raised her eyebrows. 'What does he hope to find there?'

At that moment, Holmes entered the room.

'Ah, this must be the man,' said Mary. 'I hope, sir, that you will prove that my cousin, Arthur, is innocent. I am sure that he is.'

'I agree with you, Miss Holder. And I'm sure that I will be able to prove it,' said Holmes, knocking the snow off his shoes onto the doormat. 'May I ask you a couple of questions?'

'Please do, sir, if it will help to clear up this terrible affair,' said Mary.

'Did you hear anything yourself last night? Any odd noises?' asked Holmes.

'Nothing, until my uncle began to shout,' she replied. 'Then I went to the study.'

'And you locked all the windows and doors last night?'

'Yes,' said Mary.

'And were they still locked this morning?'

'Yes.'

'You have a maid who has a sweetheart,' said Holmes. 'You told your uncle last night that she had been out to see him?'

'Yes, it was the maid who served us coffee in the drawing room yesterday evening. She may have heard Uncle mention the coronet.'

'I see,' said Holmes. 'You are suggesting that she could have gone out to tell her sweetheart about the coronet, and that

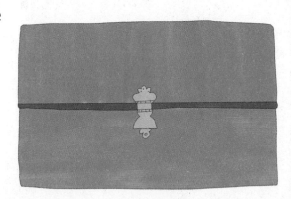

the two may have planned the robbery together.'

'What is the good of any of these theories?' asked Mr Holder impatiently. 'I have told you that I saw Arthur with the coronet in his hands!'

'Wait a moment, Mr Holder,' said Holmes. 'We will come back to that. About this girl, Miss Holder. You said that you saw her come back in by the kitchen door?'

'Yes. When I went to see if the door was locked for the night,

I saw her sneaking in. I saw the man she met, too, in the dusk,' Mary said in a hushed voice.

'Do you know him?' asked Holmes.

'Oh, yes. He's the greengrocer who delivers our vegetables. His name is Francis Prosper.'

'And he stood to the left of the door, a bit further up the path?' said Holmes.

'Yes, he did,' said Mary, a little surprised.

'And he is a man with a wooden leg?' asked Holmes.

Something like fear sprang into Mary's dark eyes. 'You are like a magician,' she said. 'How do you know that?' She smiled weakly, but Holmes did not smile in return.

'I would like to go upstairs,' he said. 'I shall probably go around the outside of the house again too. But perhaps I had better take a look at the lower windows first.'

Holmes walked quickly from one window to the other, pausing only at the large one that looked out into the stable lane. Then he

opened it and carefully examined
the sill with his magnifying glass.

'Now we shall go upstairs,' he
said at last.

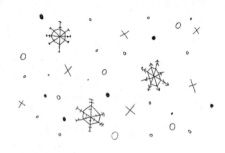

Chapter Seven

Mr Holder's study was a plainly furnished little room with grey carpet, a bookcase and a desk.

Holmes went to the desk first and looked closely at the lock.

'Which key was used to open it?' he asked.

'The one that Arthur mentioned – the one to the cupboard in the cellar. That's it on top of the bookcase,' said Mr Holder, pointing to the key.

Holmes picked it up and opened the desk. 'It's a silent lock,' he said. 'No wonder it didn't wake you.' He pulled out a round black box. 'And this box, I presume, contains the coronet? We must have a look at it.'

Holmes opened the case, took out the coronet and laid it on the table. It was a magnificent piece of jewellery – so elegant and finely crafted. The beryl stones were some of the finest I had ever seen. They were almost clear but with just a hint of blue. On one side of the coronet was a cracked edge where a point, holding three gems, had been torn away.

'Now, Mr Holder,' said Holmes. 'Please break another point off the crown.'

Mr Holder recoiled in horror.
'No. I couldn't possibly,' he said.

'Then I will.' Holmes used all
his strength trying to bend the
coronet, but he could not.

'My fingers are very strong, but I
couldn't do it,' he said. 'No ordinary
man could. Not by
himself, anyway.
You would need
the strength of two
men to break
this. And what
do you think
would happen if

I did break it, Mr Holder? There would be a noise like a gunshot. If all this happened in here, the room next to your bedroom, surely it would have woken you?'

'I don't know what to think,' said Mr Holder, clearly confused. 'It is all a mystery to me.'

Holmes turned to Mary. 'What do you think, Miss Holder?'

'I feel the same as my uncle,' said Mary.

'Mr Holder,' said Holmes. 'Was your son wearing slippers or shoes when you saw him?'

'Neither. He was wearing nothing but a shirt and trousers.'

'Thank you. I shall continue my investigations outside,' said Holmes, as he placed the coronet back into its box.

Holmes insisted on going out alone as any extra footprints would make his job more difficult. He came in again after an hour with his boots covered in snow and his expression as unreadable as ever.

'I think I have seen all there is to see, Mr Holder,' he said. 'The best thing now is for me to go back to Baker Street.'

'But the gems, Mr Holmes. Where are they?' asked Mr Holder desperately.

'I don't know,' said Holmes.

Mr Holder looked frightened. 'I shall never see them again!' he cried. 'And my son? Can you give me any hope?'

'My opinion hasn't changed,' said Holmes. 'I still think Arthur is innocent.'

'Then whatever happened in my house last night?'

Holmes put on his coat and hat. 'Please come to my rooms in Baker Street between nine and ten o'clock tomorrow morning and I shall try to make this mystery a little clearer. Are you sure that you don't mind what it costs, as long as I get the gems back?'

'Yes, sir. I would give my whole fortune for those beryls.'

'I shall look into the matter between now and then. Goodbye, Mr Holder.'

It was obvious to me that my friend had almost worked out the mystery. On the way home I tried to get him to explain it to me, but he always changed the subject. At last I gave up.

We arrived home just before three o'clock in the afternoon. Holmes hurried to his bedroom and came out again a few minutes later dressed in a ragged old coat with the collar turned up, dirty trousers, a red scarf and worn-out boots.

He looked in the mirror above the mantlepiece.

'That should do,' he said. 'I wish you could come with me, Watson, but it wouldn't work.'

He took a slice of cheese from the lunch Mrs Hudson had left us, put it between two slices of bread, and thrust it into his pocket. Then, without another word, he stepped out of the door and shut it behind him.

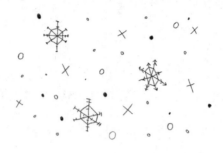

Chapter Eight

I had just finished my tea when Holmes returned.

He was whistling and swinging an old boot in his hand. Then he threw it down into a corner and helped himself to a cup of tea.

'I'm not staying,' he said. 'I'm going straight out again.' He didn't even bother to sit down at the table.

'Where to?' I asked, reaching for another scone.

'Oh, to the West End. I may be back late. Don't wait up for me,' he said cheerfully.

'How are you getting on with the investigation?'

'All right,' he said. 'I've been to Streatham again, but I didn't call at Mr Holder's house. This is a very interesting problem, Watson. I'm glad I didn't miss it. However, I mustn't sit here gossiping. I must get these awful clothes off and return to my respectable self.'

Holmes went to his bedroom and a few minutes later I heard him run downstairs, shout 'Goodbye, Watson!' and slam the front door. I sighed, disappointed that he had not asked me to go with him.

I settled myself by the fire with a book and waited for him to return. But when the clock struck midnight and there was still no sign of him, I went to bed.

I don't know what time Holmes finally came in, but in the morning there he was, sitting

at the breakfast table with a cup
of coffee in one hand and the
newspaper in the other.

'Excuse me for starting
breakfast without you, Watson,'
he said. 'But Mr Holder is coming
early this morning.'

At that moment, the clock struck nine. The cheery chime was immediately followed by the ring of doorbell. Holmes smiled. 'That will be Mr Holder, now,' he said.

I was shocked by the change in Mr Holder. His normally broad, full face now looked pale and almost sunken in at the cheeks, and his hair seemed to be a shade whiter. It was as if he had aged overnight.

He walked wearily into the room with his shoulders slumped

– just the opposite of his violent
entrance the day before. I pushed
forwards an armchair and he
dropped heavily into it.

'I don't know what I've done
to deserve this,' Mr Holder said.

'Only two days ago I was a happy and successful man without a care in the world. Now I am left lonely and ashamed. Not only is my son still in prison, but now my niece, Mary, has deserted me.'

'Deserted you?' said Holmes.

'Yes. She did not come down for breakfast this morning. When the maids went to wake her, they found that her bed had not been slept in, her room was empty, and there was a note for me on the hall table. Last night we had a row. Arthur has always been in love with Mary, and I said to her that if she had married him when he had asked, he might not have done what he did. I only meant that she would have been a good influence on him. But I shouldn't have said it,' he said miserably.

Mr Holder took a folded note out of his pocket and handed it to Holmes.

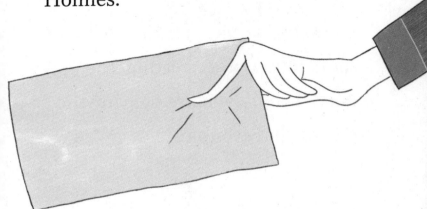

My dearest uncle,

I have brought trouble to your home, and I can never be happy here again. I must leave you forever. Don't worry about me; my future is provided for. Please don't search for me. You won't find me.

From your loving
Mary

'Perhaps this is for the best,' said Holmes after reading the note. 'I think you are nearing the end of your troubles.'

'Have you learned something?' asked Mr Holder, springing to life. 'Where are the gems?'

'Would you pay £1,000 each for the beryls?' asked Holmes, to my surprise.

'I would pay £10,000.'

'That won't be necessary, Mr Holder. £1,000 each will be enough. So £3,000 for the three beryls, plus the £1,000 reward you mentioned. That's £4,000 altogether. Please sign here to say that you'll pay. Here is a pen.'

Mr Holder looked completely dazed as he signed the paper Holmes had passed to him.

The moment he finished writing, Holmes turned around, took something out of his desk and threw it down on the table in front of us.

It was a triangular piece of gold with three gems in it. A ray of sunshine from the window caught one of the jewels and it sparkled fiercely.

Mr Holder shrieked and grabbed it. 'You have it! I am saved!'

He hugged the piece of jewellery to his chest, smiling broadly.

'There is one other thing you owe, Mr Holder,' said Holmes rather sternly.

'Owe?' Mr Holder grabbed the pen again. 'Name the sum and I will pay it.'

'The debt is not to me,' said Holmes. 'The £4,000 covered all my costs. But you do owe a very humble apology to your son.'

'It was not Arthur who took the jewels?' asked Mr Holder.

'I told you yesterday, and I repeat today, that it was not Arthur. Your son is not a thief.'

Mr Holder put his hand to his forehead. 'Then let us go to him at once and tell him that we know the truth.'

Holmes smiled. 'He knows already. When I had cleared it all up, I went to see Arthur at the police station and told him the whole story. He agreed that my theory was right and he added a few details that were not quite clear to me.'

'For heaven's sake, tell me,' said Mr Holder. 'Explain this extraordinary mystery!'

'I will tell you. But first there is something you should know. This will be hard for you to hear. Sir George Burnwell and Mary have been seeing each other. Now they have run away together.'

'My Mary? Impossible!' said Mr Holder.

'I'm afraid it is true,' said Holmes. 'Neither you nor your son knew just what kind of man Sir George was when you invited him into your home. He is one of the most dangerous men in England – a ruined gambler and a desperate villain. He is a man without heart or conscience.

'Your niece was naïve and believed him when he said that he loved her. She was flattered by his attention. He came to see her almost every evening. Then he heard about the coronet and used her to get it.'

'I cannot believe it!' said Mr Holder.

Holmes nodded as if he expected this reaction.

'Let me tell you what happened in your house that night.'

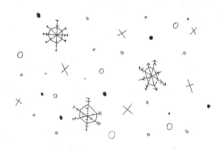

Chapter Nine

Holmes leaned back in his chair and crossed his legs.

'After you had gone to your room, Mary crept downstairs and talked to her sweetheart, Sir George, through the window that looks out onto the stable lane. She told him about the coronet and where it was hidden.

'I'm sure she loved you, Mr

Holder, but her love for Sir George was stronger. He is a charming man, as you have said, and he wanted that coronet very badly. Mary was easy to persuade. She became his partner in crime.

'When she saw you coming downstairs, she shooed Sir George away and quickly closed the window. Then she told you about the maid meeting the greengrocer, which was perfectly true. But it was all a distraction.

'Your son, Arthur, went to bed after talking to you, but he

didn't sleep well because he was worried about his gambling debts. In the middle of the night he heard quiet footsteps outside his door, so he got up and looked out. He was surprised to see Mary creeping along the hallway and disappearing into your study. Curious to see what she was doing, he put on his shirt and trousers and waited.

'After a while, she came out of the room. By the light of the hall's lamp, he saw that she was carrying the precious coronet. She went downstairs and Arthur hid behind a curtain to watch what went on in the hall below.

'He saw Mary quietly open the window, hand the coronet to someone outside, and then run back upstairs to her room. As soon as she had closed her door, Arthur knew he had to do something to save the coronet and your reputation. He rushed down and opened the window again, then climbed out into the snow in his bare feet. By the moonlight, he could see a dark figure in the lane.

The real thief, Sir George Burnwell, tried to get away, but Arthur caught him. There was a struggle as both of them tugged at the coronet. Then it suddenly snapped! Your son, finding that he had the coronet in his hands, rushed back and climbed back in through the window.

'He saw that the coronet had twisted during the fight and he was trying his hardest to straighten it, when you arrived on the scene.'

I realised that I had been holding my breath during Holmes' explanation. Mr Holder must have been too, because he gave a great sigh and said, 'Oh gosh.'

'You were very angry,' went on Holmes, 'and you accused Arthur of theft at the very moment when you should have been thanking him. Arthur said nothing about Sir George because he loved Mary and did not want to betray her.'

'And that was why she fainted when she saw the coronet!' said Mr Holder. 'Oh, what a blind fool I have been! And when Arthur asked to go outside for a few minutes, he wanted to go and

look for the missing
piece. How cruelly I
have misjudged him!'

'Indeed,' said
Holmes. 'When I arrived at the
house I walked very carefully
around it to look for marks in the
snow that might help me. First
I saw the footprints of the maid
and her sweetheart – the man
with the wooden leg – just past
the kitchen door.

'But there were no other
footprints in the garden except
those of the police, so I went

round to the stable lane. There, a very long and complex story was written in the snow before me.'

There was silence in the room. This was the part Holmes loved: revealing how he had come to his conclusions. He always dragged out the suspense.

'There was a double line of tracks, made by a man wearing

boots,' Holmes continued. 'And a second double line belonging to a man in bare feet. I was sure that these must be your son's footprints. The boot tracks had walked both ways, but the bare feet had run and overtaken the other.

'I followed the boot marks up to the hall window and then back and into the lane. I could see where the thief turned around, where he fought with Arthur, and finally, where a few drops of blood had fallen. The man in boots had then run down the lane – further on, I found more blood showing that it was he who was hurt. When I came to the main road at the other end, the footpath had been cleared of snow, so the trail ended.'

I was amazed, as usual, at Holmes' ability to read a scene as if it were a storybook.

'When I came back into the house you'll remember that I examined the windowsill with my magnifying glass,' Holmes continued. 'I could see at once that someone had climbed out of it. And there was the mark of a wet footprint of someone coming back in. I was beginning to piece together what had happened.

'But I still didn't know who the thief was. I knew that it was not you, Mr Holder, and it was not Arthur, so that only left your niece, Mary, or the maids. But if it were one of the maids, why would your son take the blame? There could only be one explanation – that it was Mary, the woman he loved. I remembered that you had seen her at the window and that she had fainted when she saw the coronet again.

'And who could be her accomplice? It must be a sweetheart, as she would not betray her family for anyone less.

I knew that she didn't go out much so she would have little chance of meeting anyone. The only person who came to your house, apart from your partner's family, was Sir George Burnwell. He was known to be untrustworthy yet charming. So I deduced that he was her accomplice.'

Mr Holder nodded.

'The next thing I did,' said Holmes, 'was dress in rags and go to Sir George's house, pretending to beg for some food at the kitchen door. From one

of the servants I learned that
Sir George had cut his head the
night before. It made me more
sure that Sir George was the true
thief, but I had to be absolutely
certain. Luckily, I spotted an
old pair of wet boots sitting by
the wall, waiting to be cleaned.

When no one was looking, I took one of them and fled. I went to your house again, Mr Holder, and matched the sole of the boot to the footprints in the snow – it fitted exactly!

'I had my man. So I went home and changed my clothes and then went to see Sir George. He denied it all at first, but when I told him all the details of the story, he knew the game was up – he could not hide the truth from me. He reached for a heavy stick, but I was too quick for him. My boxing

and martial arts experience have
made my reactions very fast.
I soon had his hands pinned
behind his back. I told him that
there was no need for violence,
as we would happily pay for the
gems he had stolen – £1,000 each.'

'"Why dash it all!" he said, angrily. "I sold all three of them for just six hundred pounds!"

'Then he gave me the name of the man he had sold them to.'

'Did you have him arrested?' I asked, eagerly.

'Sadly not, Watson. I was just about to step outside to call for a policeman when Sir George made a run for it through the opposite door. I chased after him but he knew the roads and alleyways around his home better than I did, and he escaped.

'I was annoyed, but I could not let it distract me from getting the gems back. So I went to the address Sir George had given me and, after much haggling, got the gems for £1,000 each. Then I went to see your son, Mr Holder, to tell him that he would soon be free.

'I eventually got to bed at two o'clock this morning. I call that a good day's work!'

'A day that has saved my son and has prevented a great public scandal,' said Mr Holder, standing up. 'Sir, I cannot find the words to thank you. You're more skilled than I even imagined. And now I must go to my dear boy to apologise for the wrong that I have done him. As to my poor Mary, I'm sure that not even you can tell me where she is now.'

'I think it's certain that she is with Sir George Burnwell, wherever he has gone,' said Holmes. 'In the end she will discover what kind of a man he is, and it will break her heart. That will be more than enough punishment for her part in this.

She will have learned a very hard lesson.'

Mr Holder nodded sadly and left.

Holmes rang for a pot of coffee and we settled down in front of the fire together.

After a few minutes of silence, I asked, 'Who do you think was the famous client at the bank, Holmes? The man who gave Mr Holder the beryl coronet?'

Holmes smiled. 'I think, Watson, that that is one mystery we will never know the answer to.'

Sherlock Holmes

World-renowned private detective Sherlock Holmes has solved hundreds of mysteries, and is the author of such fascinating monographs as *Early English Charters* and *The Influence of a Trade Upon the Form of a Hand*. He keeps bees in his free time.

Dr John Watson

Wounded in action at Maiwand, Dr John Watson left the army and moved into 221B Baker Street. There he was surprised to learn that his new friend, Sherlock Holmes, faced daily peril solving crimes, and began documenting his investigations.

Dr Watson also runs a doctor's practice.

To download Sherlock Holmes activities, please visit www.sweetcherrypublishing.com/resources